T0303711

More praise for *Salve*

"Harsh and beautiful, yearning and deadly, the stories of Soma Mei Sheng Frazier will remind you of nothing less than the whole wide world."

– **DANIEL HANDLER**, a.k.a. Lemony Snicket

Salve

Soma Mei Sheng Frazier

NOMADIC PRESS

OAKLAND

111 FAIRMOUNT AVENUE
OAKLAND, CA 94611

BROOKLYN

475 KENT AVENUE #302
BROOKLYN, NY 11249

WWW.NOMADICPRESS.ORG

MASTHEAD

FOUNDING AND MANAGING EDITOR
J. K. FOWLER

ASSOCIATE EDITOR
MICHAELA MULLIN

DESIGN
J. K. FOWLER

MISSION STATEMENT

Nomadic Press is a 501 (C)(3) not-for-profit organization that supports the works of emerging and established writers and artists. Through publications (including translations) and performances, Nomadic Press aims to build community among artists and across disciplines.

SUBMISSIONS

Nomadic Press wholeheartedly accepts unsolicited book manuscripts. To submit your work, please visit www.nomadicpress.org/submissions

DISTRIBUTION

Orders by trade bookstores and wholesalers:
Small Press Distribution,
1341 Seventh Street
Berkeley, CA 94701
spd@spdbooks.org
(510) 524-1668 / (800) 869-7553

Salve
© 2016 by Soma Mei Sheng Frazier

All rights reserved. No part of this book may be reproduced or transmitted in any form or by any means, electronic or mechanical, without written permission from the publisher. Requests for permission to make copies of any part of the work should be sent to: info@nomadicpress.org.

This book was made possible by a loving community of chosen family and friends, old and new.

For author questions or to book a reading at your bookstore, university/school, or alternative establishment, please send an email to info@nomadicpress.org.

Cover and back artwork by Arthur Johnstone and Livien Yin

Published by Nomadic Press, 111 Fairmount Avenue, Oakland, CA 94611

Fourth printing, 2019

Printed in the United States of America

LIBRARY OF CONGRESS CATALOGING-IN-PUBLICATION DATA

Mei Sheng Frazier, Soma, 1973 –
Title: *Salve*
P. CM.
Summary: Frazier's stories, in seamless prose, examine the myriad ways in which we soothe ourselves in an attempt to treat what ails us—for better or for worse.

[1. FICTION. 2. LOVE. 3. WOMEN AUTHORS.] I. III. TITLE.

2016934857

ISBN: 978-0-9970933-2-2

Salve

Soma Mei Sheng Frazier

NOMADIC
PRESS

for Zoe, Burgious, and Li Hua-yuan,
my heart and fists

CONTENTS

SHE MUST REMEMBER

SHE MUST REMEMBER NOT to mention her wake-and-bake-weed-smoking, jobless Carolina redneck dyke ex-lover's name. She must remember not to draw attention to the heart-shaped marinara smear on her left breast, or to her breasts at all, as the upstanding Dean of Student Affairs has already given her sheer white blouse and slightly visible black bra the stink-eye once today, guessing accurately that she dresses this way to gain an advantage over the fearless high school boys in her sophomore English class. She must remember not to show emotion, or lower her eyes, as she threads through packed hallways: shouting kids, scent of sweat, shiny narrow lockers. She must remember not to cuss like a gambler with Tourette's, staring at a 7-2 off suit hand.

The classroom is yellow with sunlight. This is not a typical secondary school; rather, an elite private institution in a renovated 1920's art deco hotel, all high ceilings and marble bathrooms and dark wood doors.

She must remember that the quiet one is Juliette—for the quiet ones become allies quickly, before the louder ones realize that they love her too; that she is their favorite teacher because she lets them talk. She must remember to let them talk: not while completing assignments, but in the brief moments after the bell rings, when the French financier's daughter catches her by the sleeve, *Ms. Katz*, to tell her how that late-night party, where she ended up the last girl drinking vodka with boys she had thought were her friends, went wrong; or in the early morning, before class, when the football Center who threatened to toss the algebra tutor out the third-floor window is waiting for her with a loaf of banana bread he's baked himself. *Thank you for explaining comma splices without getting mad. You never talk to me like I'm dumb.* She must remember, too, that the charismatic mother of the sociopathic Louisiana implant exploited a tragedy—got her son into the school by claiming he'd been a straight A student at a school whose records were wiped out in the hurricane, though it was perfectly clear he'd never cracked a book in his life.

The faculty lounge is intimate and warm, connected to an oak paneled reading room and a miniature library. In the library, a classic rolling ladder allows her to reach the topmost shelves, and motes of dust float incessantly, year-round, on some soft current that circulates from nowhere.

She must remember not to mention her wake-and-bake-weed-smoking, jobless Carolina redneck dyke ex-lover's name. She must remember to label her Cokes, or lose them to the Dean of Discipline. She must remember not to grin as she watches the Coke thief rummage through the faculty fridge, and imagines the contents of his desk drawers: riding crop, paddle, ball gag, nipple clamps, leather gimp suit, hose? She must remember that the Assistant Headmaster is a widow who insists on *Mrs.* although, if the gossip here is to be trusted, she hated her husband, may he rest in peace, and slept around.

The Rockefeller Room: long conference table, hidden modern lighting, and subtle ivory walls hung with stiff portraits of past headmasters. She likes to sneak in there and stare blankly out the window overlooking the quad, when it's not booked for board meetings (uppity powwows at which manicured suits grip and grin and say things like *I don't want to ant-fuck about formatting* and *tell that idiot bean-counter to get me the goddamn budget* to prove they're still men, or can play ball with the men).

She must remember not to mention her wake-and-bake-weed-smoking, jobless Carolina redneck dyke ex-lover's name. She must remember that it is an honor, and not a fucking pain in the ass time-suck, that keeps her at work late the first Monday of every month, to sit as the sole faculty member on the Fundraising Committee and strategize about how to help a bunch of rich assholes get more money out of their rich asshole friends and contacts. She must remember that she was hired—and for more than even the most seasoned teachers are generally paid—as much for her West Coast connections to wealthy potential donors as for her impressive curriculum vita. She must remember not to push too hard on behalf of the scholarship students: *we really need to provide a study-abroad experience for Amara, because all of the other kids' parents have access to such resources and . . .* She must remember to wear the sheer white blouse and slightly visible black bra on the first Monday of next month—that is, if she can get the marinara out.

The detention hall is actually just the well-appointed dining hall, transformed by the magic of the last bell. The solid, dark wood table at which she sits with the sociopathic Louisiana implant is engraved with furtive carvings: *Maya LOVES Adam* and *Fucking Dean Dickwad can lick my scrot'.* (She is impressed by the apostrophe.)

She must remember not to mention her wake-and-bake-weed-smoking, jobless Carolina redneck dyke ex-lover's name. She must remember to convey the egregiousness and foolishness of stealing another student's ideas, and presenting them in a portfolio that was to have been shared with the class, while avoiding ambiguous or incendiary language that this kid's charismatic mom can use to get her fired before the rest of the faculty discerns that he's a sociopath—they've been had by a teenage con and his well-heeled con mom—and he quietly transfers to another school. She must remember the name of the rapidly promoted black New York Times journalist who was fired for plagiarism, in one blow decimating his own career and discrediting affirmative action, at least in the eyes of the reactionary right. She must remember to clarify that there is also a reactionary left, leaving her personal politics obscure. She must remember why she broke up with her wake-and-bake-weed-smoking, jobless Carolina redneck dyke ex-lover.

The parking lot is nearly empty under a vast cobalt sky. It was for her own safety and prosperity, right—not just a thankless future at a snooty school where payday rolled around and most of the faculty lined up to have shit tossed at them?

She must remember not to mention her wake-and-bake-weed-smoking, jobless Carolina redneck dyke ex-lover's name. She must remember that the Director of Institutional Advancement position will open up next week as the current, incompetent director is fully phased out. She must remember not to interrupt *Mrs.* Assistant Headmaster's diatribe about having to stay late to reprimand a scholarship student's single mom for the misplaced values that led her to refuse to miss work at a *gas station* to attend *vital* PTA meetings with the other, *quality* mothers who *care* about their children's *wellbeing* for goodness' sake. She must remember that nobody here could possibly guess how her own mother had raised her on bodega soda pop and boxed spaghetti, the two of them hustling to pay the rent on a South Bronx efficiency apartment; that her wealthy West Coast connections are comprised of strangers she researched online; that her curriculum vita is a lie and she can always spot the cheaters because she's just like them: doesn't give a damn about the rules that invisible people with power drafted; just wants these assholes to pay her an increasingly ridiculous guilt fee to pay attention to their kids; can't believe a father could avoid raising his daughter to the extent that she thought a home office packed with plastered, entitled, savage teenage boys constituted a fun, safe evening among friends.

The Englander—a stereotype of a pub where the school's administrators get sotted and dish goss about the faculty while the faculty, in an adjacent room, get arseholed and gab about the administrators—is too warm. An apply scent hangs in the cloying air, reminding her of her diabetic amputee uncle Garth, buried in Saint Raymond Cemetery.

She must remember not to mention her wake-and-bake-weed-smoking, jobless Carolina redneck dyke ex-lover's name. She must remember to stick with ale and forego the hard stuff till she's alone, at home, in her black bra and pajama pants. She must remember to be acerbically witty; and to balance that with empathic nodding when her sloshed coworkers start shit-talking the young people they've opted to teach. She must remember to hit the loo and soap the heart-shaped stain out of her blouse, before it sets in. She must remember to prolong eye contact with the headmaster's assistant, Ringo, who actually does look like a British pop star and drinks with the faculty despite having the ear of the icy, erudite board member heading up the Hiring Committee. She must remember to hit the hard stuff and soap out the memory of her wake-and-bake-weed-smoking, jobless Carolina redneck dyke ex-lover's name, before it sets in—

The kitchen is her favorite room; possibly her favorite place in the entire world. Its peeling walls still hold the soft scent of her ex-lover's fried hush puppies, and there's vodka nestled in the freezer between frozen peas and more vodka.

She must remember me. She must remember something of the way I gently held her face, like a good mother does her baby's, and kissed her tears away.

The bathroom is too bright. She leans close to the mirror and suddenly realizes she is beautiful, as she does every time she drinks slightly too much ale at the Englander.

She must remember that I need this role, this deception, to ascend socially whereas she, much stronger, is free from the urge to climb.

The bed is soft. Welcoming.

She must remember how hard we fought, and that fights among equals can never be won.

The light is off; the room airy and dark.

She must remember that—though the world is full of trap-doors and idiots will hear her accent and smell the weed that helps her eat despite the chemo and mistake *her* for the idiot and gorgeous teenage girls are brutally gang-raped at late-night parties on the leather couches of their financier fathers' home offices and good mothers are compared unfavorably with bad ones, and people leave one another, even when they love them, maybe especially when they love them—somebody saw her once, eye to eye, and found her lovely.

ZERO PRESSURE

SICKLE CELL IS NOT just a black disease. Though this fact has been public for decades, people still startle when they find out that I have it. It's like the year is 1983 and I've just introduced myself as Gaëtan Dugas, the promiscuous gay flight attendant who was North America's first known AIDS carrier. Sometimes they lean away, or wipe their palms against their slacks if we've shaken hands.

Another little-known fact is that sickle cell is extremely painful. Imagine sticky, microscopic scythes catching on the insides of your blood vessels and clogging them up. These little weapons are your red blood cells after they've elongated into sickles, which happens periodically throughout your life when your arterial oxygen pressure dips too low.

Once stuck, the cells stop transporting oxygen to the various parts of your body. You can see how the risks multiply from there. If enough cells sickle during an attack, they'll cause the vessels to warp and collapse. Worse, prolonged oxygen deprivation in your bones and organs can mean necrosis. Even if you never suffer from the most severe complications, which include stroke, brain damage and penile infarction, you live in fear of them.

The disease also brings the stigma of visible sores. For years black Americans used to cover up their sickle cell lesions with tar soap. I'm a 31-year-old white man named Jim Thibodeaux who can handle physical pain, but the tar soap story haunts me because every summer I play volleyball with my employees while secretly worrying about the makeup my wife buys me melting off my ulcerated legs.

In those moments I remind myself of three facts: One, I have a brilliant, gorgeous wife. Two, I'm not even 35 and I own a successful travel business—and not, by the way, an inherited one. Three, other than the chronic leg sores, I haven't really been affected by my disease except when it comes to commuting. I can't even book puddle-jumpers for short flights because long before a plane reaches 68,000 feet, where the air pressure is just about zero, I risk a severe attack. Jet cabins are pressurized but small planes' cabins aren't. My blood cells can't handle that, so I end up taking a lot of trains for business.

The most universal symptom of sickle cell, which I try not to think about, is a shortened life-span. Before the medical community had a grasp on the disease, Africans called it ogbanjes, meaning "children who come and go," because if you got it you weren't sticking around for long. Now, odds are I'll see 40 or even 45.

I never see much literature or information out there about the disease, maybe because it isn't contagious so the authorities figure why bother. Premature death is the one symptom that seems to be commonly known. I'm not fond of sympathy but I do appreciate a rudimentary level of understanding. Of course a little knowledge can be a dangerous thing too: for a while, the US government forced all black Air Force applicants to undergo testing for the sickle cell mutation. Before finally getting sued, they dismissed 143 applicants who didn't actually have the disease but had inherited a defective allele from one parent, making them genetic carriers. That was a long time ago, in the 1970s, but still.

I know a lot of these little factoids because my wife, Lauren, is a history teacher. She works at Oakland Academy of the Arts, which is not just an art school but also a prep school. A few years back, when my business really picked up, Lauren was feeling burnt out and considered quitting her job—but she decided to stay so that, should one of our future children turn out to be artistic, we'd have an in at the school. OAA is extremely selective.

Now it looks like Lauren's tenacity may be rewarded. We're pregnant with a baby girl. I used to think that only cheesy men used the term "we're pregnant," but not anymore. Last week during the ultrasound, our daughter waved her right hand at us as if saying hello. If I could carry her in my own body I would. I'd even give birth to her when the time comes, because as I said I can handle physical pain. It wasn't always that way, but a positive side effect of sickle cell is that you learn not to let the pain get to you. Other than that, the only upside is that you're far less likely to die from malaria, so go on, take that exotic vacation and forget the mosquito netting.

My only fear about giving birth would be the possibility of post-partum depression. Pain that attacks your body is one thing but I watched my sister go through eight months of depression after having her first boy. She would sit with her nose inches away from the living room window in her high-rise condo, pretending to watch the neighborhood, but then the sun would set and she would still be sitting there long after the window was empty of its pretty picture and only reflected her sad face.

For me the worst phase of post-partum might be beforehand, wondering whether I was going to get it. I hate that kind of murky foreboding feeling. It's been a little like that for us throughout Lauren's pregnancy, because my wife carries the sickle cell trait although she doesn't have the disease. Around her two month mark, we were scheduled to go in for a prenatal screening. There was a 50% chance that the test would say our baby had the disease and a 50% chance that it would tell us she was just a carrier, like Lauren.

We stayed up late the night before the appointment, fighting, and in the morning we didn't go. Instead we made a deal that each of us would sign up for individual therapy to really get a grip on the situation. We reached this decision after a debate about how we would handle things if our daughter had the disease, followed by two hours of Lauren crying and panicking in our small warm kitchen, and me sitting there silently.

In the three years that we've been married, which have also been the three happiest years of my life, I've uttered barely a word to my wife during a fight. This may sound cruel, but what I'm trying to do, with all my might, is avoid saying anything stupid while she's already upset. During our very first fight as an engaged couple I spoke up, and I've spent the four years since wishing I hadn't. The fight had started out as a goofy sparring match around what we might one day name our future children, and ended with Lauren calling me racist.

Lauren, like most sickle cell carriers, is black.

Anyway the day of our scheduled prenatal appointment we woke up exhausted, returned to the kitchen with the phone book, and signed up with separate shrinks. She's iffy about hers but I like mine. My therapist's name is Alan M. Rapp. When I walked in for our initial appointment, admiring the fact that he could practice in a flower-filled office and wear a yellow plaid shirt while still retaining an admirable amount of benevolent masculinity, he said: "Call me Al." Later in the session, during a quiet moment in which I examined his credentials on the wall, Al's other nickname occurred to me. I glanced sharply from the framed certificates to his face, and he gave a slow, knowing smile that caused creases to appear around his eyes and mouth. "Yes," he said, "some folks call me Shrink Rapp."

I see Al every week now. Sometimes we talk about sickle cell and fatherhood but mostly, surprisingly, it's about Lauren. I have never been a man who talks about women with other men—particularly not about Lauren—but in doing so with Al, I've learned three things. First, ever since I found out that she was a sickle cell carrier, shortly after we got serious, I've been angry with her. Second, I love her more than anything and will get over my anger.

The other lesson I've learned is that anger and fear are basically the same thing. Minus one letter, they're even the same word: fight/flight. This helps me out a lot. Maybe the next time Lauren cries, which hopefully won't be soon, I'll be able to remember it, calm myself down and say a few cautious words.

As challenging as remembering new things can be, forgetting them has been harder lately. I want to forget about the disease and live my life around it again, rather than inside it—but every time I look at my wife's belly, I remember. When I pick her up from work I find myself wandering toward the reference section of the school library, where a few hardbound red medical books huddle together on a metal shelf. Then, while Lauren is inevitably held up by a parent or student, I learn a little more about sickle cell, and every new piece of information reminds me of Gaëtan Dugas.

Mr. Dugas, the infamous AIDS carrier, was a white guy like me, with French-Canadian roots like mine, who died of his terminal illness when he was my age. They say he left 2,500 sexual partners strewn in his flight path. When he felt well, he used makeup to cover his lesions but when he was gloomy, he made a point of displaying them to the other flight attendants. "I have the gay cancer," his colleagues quoted him as saying in despondent moments, as he counted his purple sores. "Maybe you'll get it too."

I haven't mentioned this to Al yet but every time I drive past Lauren's school now, or leave the obstetrician's office, I become Gaëtan Dugas. It's not like I'm comparing my sexual roster to his or sickle cell to AIDS, but I've always remembered something that Lauren told me: in the AIDS community, Mr. Dugas is known as Patient Zero.

When I start to get these weird empathic pangs, my own identity fades out. I cease to be a happy, successful, expectant father with a study to paint pink and fresh new problems to solve—like how to raise a girl up to be a soccer player instead of a cheerleader. Suddenly I'm a dying, pestilent man who should have been more careful in choosing a partner himself. Then it begins to feel like I'm not even a man anymore, but just a dumb disease that will eventually kill its host, negate itself. A zero. I start to scratch at the crusted sores on my legs, the blood drains from my head and the pain starts up as though I'm climbing toward 68,000 feet in the sky. Usually at that point, if I'm alone, I pull the car to the side of the road.

Just before I cross the horizon, black out, disappear, I force myself to breathe deep breaths and remember the deep connection between fear and anger. I remember Al's crinkly grin, which tells me that he's a good guy who genuinely likes me because I'm a good guy too. Then I think about Lauren's delicate shoulders, slender hips and big pregnant belly, and finally I let myself remember the missed prenatal appointment.

That morning we sat in the kitchen holding hands across the table. Before the pregnancy, we'd bought supplies and repainted the kitchen a nice color: champagne, it's called, and so of course we drank a bottle while we worked and the edging's a little uneven in the corner where Lauren finished up. There's a square, burnished steel clock on the wall near that corner. I was facing it as we sat at the table, and I watched our prenatal screening hour come and go. During this time Lauren found her shrink and set an appointment. Then she hung up the phone and put her hands inside mine again.

By now I had my apology ready. I was about to speak when Lauren blinked hard a couple of times, swallowed, rubbed her forehead and started apologizing to me—not just about the night before, but also for our first fight, four years ago, when she'd called me racist. She swore that she never would have married me if I were a racist. Her grandma would have killed her, 87 years old or not. She gave a little dry laugh. That fight wasn't actually about names, heritage or racism, she said, and last night's fight wasn't about how we would raise our daughter together.

"It's just the opposite, Jimmy."

I stared at her. "The opposite?"

"I'm terrified. I don't want to raise a child alone after you die." Her hands were cold and I rubbed them slowly with my thumbs. "Fear comes out in weird ways sometimes, Jimmy," she said. Then she opened her eyes wide for a moment, shut them tight, dropped her head and started crying as though it were she who was killing me and not the disease. I had to let go of her hands so she could wipe her face.

I do some deep breathing in the car while I replay what my wife said, shift in my seat and roll down the driver's side window. That was a hard thing to hear. It may have thrown me off a little, but as with the physical pain, I'm pretty sure I'm learning how to handle this new Patient Zero phenomenon. I picture Lauren walking down our driveway with her arm around a healthy, grinning girl in a soccer uniform. I remind myself that the sum of one's existence is counted in blessings and not in years, and then, slowly, I count. I count my blessings: wife, job, happiness. Baby.

Slowly my hollow center fills in, the pain weakens and my feelings about that morning revert to life size. I keep my breathing steady and remind myself that rescheduling the screening won't change anything, since it's not a treatment or a cure; only a test, like the test of being able to forgive yourself and the people you love.

While the panic dissipates, I breathe strong breaths and envision genius angels in white lab coats, who for some reason look like Groucho Marx. They move efficiently around me as I sit in their laboratory in the clouds. They're busy improving bone marrow transplantation and gene therapy procedures, and handing each medical advance down to the earthly doctors who will treat my daughter after I die. That's if she even inherits the disease. 50% is better odds than life generally gives you; better than they give you in Vegas.

At that point I can pull back into traffic, concentrate on the road. I'm me again: a successful, married young business owner who will soon have a baby daughter. It's like I've hit zero pressure and come back down. I can see the ground below, make out the details of the earth in proportion to the sky, and my flight path is clear. Sometimes then I have a fleeting image of Gaëtan Dugas. He looks at me closely, not smiling or frowning, just before his name leaves my thoughts. In its place come other names, like Malika. Serena. Rose.

FLYAWAYS

I'M NOT AN OLD woman anymore, but a crisp leaf snapping loose. In the Brooklyn garden there were tall black oaks; the scent of soil, hinting at autumn. I toiled on all fours while the neighborhood kids planted rag-and-broom scarecrows amid scrawny tomato plants. Now the garden is a memory, replaced by a lively café, and the sun leans white-hot across the pillow where I wait for the wind to catch me. They're all here, my three children, but the girl's gone off to get coffee. 2013. I turn my head from the sky beyond the windowpane; grasp the bed's cool, mechanical rails. I'll wait.

2000. My daughter finds joy in scrutinizing the garden—not in the same way I do, separating leaves to reveal new sprouts, but from a distance. These are the early, self-righteous days of her ex-pat status, and from her Vancouver kitchen Penelope reads me an opinion piece on American gentrification. The rant examines the mistakes that well-intentioned, upwardly mobile U.S. citizens make in cleaning up urban neighborhoods whose primary industries are *runnin girls, slangin weed and hittin licks*.

"That's prostitution, drug dealing and robbing liquor stores, Mom," Penelope explains—perhaps forgetting that I've lived in New York for seventy-two years.

"Pen." I push the phone tightly to my ear, as though it might bring her closer. "Don't you remember our neighborhood? It's never needed cleaning up. It's always been lovely." Her tongue clucks, and I hear a sharp exhalation. "Your high school friends carved jack-o-lanterns in our community garden."

"Sure," she says, closing the conversation. "America's perfect. And if there are problems, rutabaga and chard will fix them."

Of course, that was long before this: long before I was a dry leaf, separating from the hodgepodge family tree that Pen once traced from fall foliage. Mom, the oak leaf. Dad, the birch. The brother who shared her room, flowering dogwood. The brother in my belly, American beech.

In the past thirteen years, the children have gentled—and this week, they're downright timid. They've stopped using words like "survive," "fight back" and "beat this thing." Now they say "relax," "lie back" and "be comfortable." I bob up and down on the memory of a brown crayon branch. I ride morphine, scopolamine, diazepam, methotrimeprazine. Being unmoored isn't great, but it's better than seizures and pain.

She's not a young woman anymore, but the hospital makes her feel like a child. She remembers her mother trailing her gurney to the operating room when she was twelve, and her appendix burst. Ten, nine, eight, seven, the anesthesiologist counted, and she was out like a light. When she woke up and asked where her daddy was, her mother gave a curt nod. "He's at home, Pen," she said, "too scared to see you in pain."

1976. My own mother is sixty-eight, nearly two decades younger than I am now. Yet in her memory she's seventeen and pregnant. I'm not her secret dream and my father's niggling anxiety anymore, but an actual fetus with an actual heartbeat, and she imagines that she feels my quiet cadence. Seated on the edge of her Naugahyde couch, I perch at her elbow listening.

It's 1928 and my young parents hold hands, navigating Jazz Age Manhattan. Plumes rise from the city beneath the city—twist up around their ankles as they weave away from the shabby examination room. Their fingers are interlocked, their thoughts distant and abstracted. They want to speak about what they've just done, hightailing it out of a back-alley clinic, but they're overwhelmed. Their parents know nothing of this. Rank vapors spill from under the streets, and the baby accompanies them unseen, like a ghost.

"Instead of a ghost," Mama corrects herself thoughtfully. "We'd thought it would go a different way." She shrugs. "But when the doctor told us how big you might already be, to prepare us, we couldn't. We couldn't go through with—" She places a firm hand on my knee, as though I might still fear termination. In his library down the hall, my father coughs.

An hour later, I leave my folks' apartment. I push the elevator's L button several times. Finally it drops me off, and I rush outside. Why has my mother waited this long to tell me my origin story? She's always been a private woman—played her cards close to the vest. Perhaps she assumed I'd resent her?

Thank you, Mama, I think instead; thanks for keeping me around. I stride toward Broadway, passing Genuine U.S. Government Surplus Rifles Swords Ammo, Manny's Treasures, Marie's Beauty Lounge, Welcome to Sunset Junction. I'll take the Brighton Beach line home.

On its surface, Manhattan has changed since my parents were teens: the people, the noises, the fashions, the food. Yet the same leaky pipes usher steam under the reinvented city to operate laundries, heat and cool buildings, sterilize medical equipment. I can smell the ubiquitous steam—I turn in my hospital bed—

It's bright again, or still. My sons are in the same clothes as before, but that doesn't mean anything. A day may well have passed, or several. Settling on my side, I send love to my parents; to the memory of that exhilarated, scared young couple. I go to them again.

Daddy and Mama, and I in her belly, walk past a vivid green park. He glances up at a boy in a tree: leather shoes scrabbling uncertainly at the trunk. He can't take his eyes off of the child's grasping fingers; the mother's steady presence beneath his small feet. He looks so long that he stumbles on the sidewalk, and my mother squeezes his hand. He nods: I'm okay.

Porgy, a theater poster reads, *A noisy, brilliant Negro tragedy*. They pass storefronts and restaurants. Ottomonelli & Sons.

Still today—like us, their inhabitants—the boroughs strive to reinvent themselves. Only their ancient, leaky pipes tell the truth: New York's façade is modern, but its innards are not. Even glittering Manhattan is just an old house with twenty coats of paint.

A doctor calls out in the hallway, bringing me halfway back. The open door of my room is smudged, and I remember what my husband said once back in Brooklyn, when I questioned paying the neighborhood boys good money (again) to repaint our tired stoop. "Look at that door—that doorframe," he barked proudly. "Fresh paint's like those dick drugs they're pushing nowadays. Gives new life to old wood!" Winking: "Let me handle the house, Lovey, and I'll pick up a prescription." Always, he'd shock me into agreeing. Twenty-one coats—twenty-two coats—twenty-three coats of paint—

I borrow a move from Arthur's playbook. "My throat's tight as my asshole," I croak. This gets my sons' attention with a flair: it's not something that their mother would say. Who is the scrappy figure in the automated bed? Nervously, they draw close. One pours water in my lightweight paper cup. (Whoever imagines, while young, that lifting a ceramic mug may one day prove as impossible a proposition as steadying Sisyphus's boulder?) I proffer a motherly smile. "Where's Penelope?" When the boys stay silent, I ask instead: "Where's the coffee machine?"

"Venus," says Artie.

"Pluto," says his brother.

She's not getting coffee anymore, she realizes, but taking an extended tour of the facility. Along one wall, a tasteful glass display vaunts the names of philanthropic donors. Along another runs a photographic collage of newborn babies. Realizing that the hallways in her mother's wing are bare, she envisions a collage of coffins.

I'm not a baby anymore, but a shrieking girl on stout limbs escaping my father's fingertips before bed as he gives chase through the living room. Upsetting and living up to expectations, my parents are in their twenties now, married and still in love.

1933. I see Daddy only briefly, for two minutes in the morning and an hour or so at night, but it's him I love best—despite my mother's constant care, her practical wisdom; despite the way she takes charge when I catch the sharp edge of the bookshelf and our wild chase ends. Walking me over to the brass floor lamp, first aid kit in hand, she tells my father to sit and breathe. She daubs my screaming face to clean the gash; closes my forehead with a bandage, pulling the ragged edges barely together so the scar will come out smooth.

This moment, crying up into my mom's concentrated stare and glancing occasionally over at my father, who's crumpled on the couch, will become my clearest memory of my parents: clearer than the days that Daddy took off of work, bundling us into the car to hit Coney Island; clearer than the way we huddled together, three cold bodies laughing and then snoring, on winter nights in their feather bed. And because the memory is so clear (something to do with adrenaline and shock) I'll replay it over and over, and the scar on my forehead will become a talisman of warmth and safety that I touch, even now, at this late hour when—

—the boys stand over me, pushing at my lips with something. What do they want? I sip; feel my throat relax and cool. Artie, second-eldest and another ex-pat, is a veterinarian with a Costa Rican wife and children. Robert, the youngest, is a City Attorney practicing law in service of the public—jus pro populo—because Oakland, he claims, needs justice.

1984. "It's crazy here, Mom," he gushes during a long-distance call. "More criminals in City Hall than the city's jails."

"Overall, though, California's sane? Mellow?"

"Not so much as you'd think. Let me describe our state flag. It's a fucking grizzly, Mom, striding angrily toward a blood-red star." The flag, he explains, originated in 1846 when American settlers stole the City of Sonoma from the Mexican government. "They renamed it The Republic of California. Needed a new flag to fly. They were ranchers, farmers and drifters, so the flag they made was crude—but it served its purpose. 'We're vicious,' it told the Mexican authorities. 'Vicious as bears!'"

Periodically, after that conversation, I've thought of the Californian flag when recalling the boys' gruff teenage years. The settlers flew it for a month before adopting the stars and stripes.

Now I wonder about my sons; how much gruffness they've managed to retain. Do their colleagues take advantage? Their friends? The room is bright; oppressively quiet despite the propped door. Robert tosses my empty cup in the trash. Artie bends to readjust the bedding. "Let go of the bedrail here, Mom," he says, prying at my grip, but I hang on tight.

She's not in the hospital anymore, but some kind of courtyard. While the summer sun is hot, it's cool and damp here, shaded by buildings. A man with one leg and one arm beckons her over to a bench. "Sit down and let me tell you about Honduras," he says. "We've got personnel stationed there, at Soto Cano Airbase, that nobody even remembers. Iraq, Afghanistan, Africa—" he throws his hand up in the air and waves it around "—nobody talks about Palmerola or JTF-Bravo, of which—" the wave ends in a flourish "—ya boy here was a major part." He tells her about emergency evacuations and drug lords; helping train Honduran military, police and fire agencies. Although she isn't quite sure what to believe, she listens for a half-hour, soothed by forgetting her mother: soothed to learn that Honduras suffers a deplorable homicide rate; that its government is losing a war with transnational organized crime. "We deployed some Seals over there to help create an elite unit," he says, "but that won't shut down the drug traffickers. Nothing will. It's a booming business—and Honduran maritime special forces don't know shit about shit." He points, with his hand, to his absent limbs. "And neither do we goddammit."

1953. I'm not a straight girl anymore, but a woman with a secret. Under a 10th Street fire escape, Magdalena whispers in my ear. Dark and tall, she's new to New York. We met earlier at a party; broke out alone. I've never wanted another woman before.

Touching my elbow, my hip, she discloses how her mother and father died in a train accident when she was just five. Her grandparents shipped her off to Tennessee, to live with a podiatrist uncle who was also a Grand Dragon of the Klan.

The telling is punctuated by rough breath, grazing skin: how she fled Johnson City at thirteen and made it as far as West Virginia before her uncle caught up; how, furious during the long drive back, he didn't touch her—but she constantly feared that he would. How did he not, I think shamefully. How could anyone not touch her at all?

My fingertips investigate the give of her throat and the hard bones of her wrists, much smaller than a man's, as she describes ten more years in the South. "I was afraid all the time," she whispers. "That's why I'm fearless now. I'll never leave New York."

"Is your uncle still alive?" I roll my hot forehead against her cool one.

"Yes."

"What does he do?"

"Same things. Look at feet. Serve as Secretary of the Cabinet of Conservative Citizens." A moist breeze plucks at her char black hair, lifting strands. "I need a place to stay." She presses a palm into the small of my back, and that's it. She's it: my life's single consuming passion, till Penelope—such a different kind of love. Children force you to grow shrewd and kind. Lena made me sloppy and mean.

I lead her to my overheated apartment, where the radiator's noise punctuates our soft sounds. Makeshift ashtrays overflow with Chesterfields, stacked hatboxes form a wobbly coffee table, and we kiss and fight and kiss and fight, and I believe this is heaven.

When she leaves five weeks later, headed home to the South that she ran from, I discover the closet. I open the door, step in, and shut it firmly behind me.

Under Palliative Care's soft, institutional sheets I worry about this. Should I have told Pen, Artie and Robert about Lena—just to let them know it would be okay; that I would love whomever they loved, without question? Is it such a different time, a different place, that we live in today? Or has virulent hatred persisted like the city underneath the city—its hidden machinations existing now as they did then? Leaking up into our air.

The first night without Lena, I sleep poorly under twisted sheets. I resolve to want men and only men, because even in the Village—hangout of Allen Ginsberg, William S. Burroughs, James Baldwin and Marianne Moore—a bisexual woman isn't safe. I push my nose into Lena's pillow, capturing her scent inside my chest. I can't imagine a life without her, but that's the life I'll build. And quickly.

Arthur? Dear Arthur, who'll love me faithfully and boisterously till the heart attack fells you, I'll meet you just days from now. And you will make my life bearable. You will make my life good. Because people make choices like this every day. 1453, 1753, 1953: painters give up painting. Sailors let go of the sea.

Arthur, my best friend, my husband, my birch leaf—wait. I'll be there soon. Our children have stopped saying "treatment" and "tomorrow." Now they say "What do you need us to do?"

She's not outside anymore, but creeping along a corridor that perhaps she shouldn't be in. She turns a corner and finds herself behind two orderlies. Trailing them stealthily, she winds up back in the oncology building, close to Palliative Care.

1985. I'm not a housewife anymore, but a career woman gunning for retirement. All of my children have grown up and flown away, off to faraway cities. Vancouver, Oakland, Puerto Limón. They send crowded postcards to my high-ceilinged office. I write back with updates about their father (who's always the same) and my thirty-year-old supervisor, Jimmy.

"Kai looks like an angel," Jimmy blurted out at last night's mandatory holiday party. Kai's the new intern. (Hosted bar. We were all in fine form.) Later, he tried to clarify that he'd meant "ethereal, untouchable," which is a lie. He wants to mount that Christmas angel on his tree.

I scratch this out and write something more innocuous: *Your father's bathroom reading tastes have shifted from world history to nautical adventures.*

At one point, my sole aim was to amuse the children—make them laugh, so they'd keep coming back. But finally, knocking on sixty's door, I've matured into some kind of role model. Satisfied with no more promotions. Balancing home and work. Throwing tame dinners. Making fewer snarky observations. The children assume that my mind has dulled—but no matter, I tell myself. In a shallow and skeptical world, somebody's got to model kindness.

Standing over the glowing machine in the low-lit

copy room, I duplicate the letter twice. Last week, Jimmy caught me photocopying a personal bank statement. "Is that an appropriate use of company funds?" he asked, putting on his serious face.

I slip the three sheets in envelopes, the original addressed to Penelope as always, run them through the company's postal meter, and drop them in Outgoing Mail.

Back in my office, I finger the fuzzy corner of Pen's latest postcard: a black and white shot of an empty canoe drifting offshore. I store her cards at the bottom of the drawer, beneath my two sons', to obfuscate the fact that she's my favorite. Several afternoons a week, though, I dig one out and reread it. There are hundreds. *Why waste your time writing cards to the one person who understands you're too busy*, I think when I'm generous and happy. *Why crowd a card*, I think, when I'm not: *why not compose a real letter?*

The canoe rocks gently, gently.

She's not sure anymore: what to do, where to go. All she knows is that she needs to get back to her mother's bedside and can't. Not just yet. In a flash, she remembers her own hospital bed—one of six in the sunny recovery room where she woke up, age twelve, sans appendix. Her whole body heats and she begins to sweat as, instantaneously, she forgives her father for not having been there.

I'm not a grandmother anymore but a leaf, a leaf, dancing around the lollipops: those round white springtime flowers that Penelope nicknames as we stroll down Emmons Avenue. "Aren't they sweet, Mommy? Little lollipop candies for the bees."

1959. Her eyes flash up at me; small hand finds mine. At four years old, she's just a fragile bud herself. I gaze down at her narrow back as she stops sporadically, bending over the edges of lawns and schoolyards to examine their bounties of candy. Artie, Jr. is at his grandparents' and Robert, in my belly. We have no place to be until dinnertime, I think, and then: No Place is a town in England. This is an odd fact that I learned when I was Pen's age—though I've no idea where. The town's name may be a shortening of "North Place," I remember, but historians aren't certain.

Penelope pulls me here and there, delighted, and my mind meanders too. We pass 99 Cent Variety, Copy Ship Passport Pix & Notary, Chuchifritos Frituras BBQ. Buzz buzz buzz go the bees in their white lollipops. Buzz buzz buzz goes the equipment in the corner. Buzz. Buzz. Buzz. Buzz. Buzz. The nurses tread noiselessly, but the doctors' shoes squeak as they enter and leave.

She's not Penelope anymore, but a confused and isolated stranger hiding between the Oncology and Palliative Care, in the gray cement stairwell where the nurses smoke. Her husband and daughter are back in Vancouver. Somehow, together, the three of them had conspired to pretend that this visit wouldn't be the last. "We'll fly down with you next time," Jarrod had said casually. "Your Mom's a fighter." And it's true—but this isn't a winnable war. Is any war winnable, she wonders, remembering the man in the courtyard—or does war beget war beget war? And why are Canadians so goddamned optimistic? Her coffee is long gone. She rolls the tip of her shoe across a cluster of cigarette butts. 4:10 pm. She heads back.

I'm not a person anymore, but a combination of symptoms and failings—mind scattershot. In the children's ward there are puppies. Why not a puppy for me? Half a liver for a lick, and a tongue for a tail. "Swallowing anything—even water—may break the spots on her tongue open. And ingesting blood will increase her nausea. We need to make a few more decisions." At this stage, Doctor, what? Cut my tongue out like a mob boss, and send it to my husband? *Snitches get stitches*, the card will read, but it'll only come back in the mail. I lie on my belly, face hidden in brittle hair, till the palliative specialist leaves.

The boys are talking about the bear on California's flag. Perhaps I've been thinking aloud? "His name is Monarch," Robert says. "He's a real, taxidermied grizzly that California used as a model when we readopted the flag in 1911."

His brother nods. There's a metallic scent in the room. My right foot pokes out of the blanket, bluish and cold. I recall asking Artie to remove my socks. "They kept him in a concrete cage when he was alive, as a publicity stunt. In photos he looked pretty despondent. And you can still visit him today, on display in the basement of the Academy of Sciences—" from an adjacent room, a sudden alarm "—though he's a little worse for the wear." Robert falls silent. They listen to the urgent beeping.

Doctors swarm the wing; rush past our open door. Down the hallway, another door closes and the alarm is muted or stopped. The boys exchange a look, while avoiding looking at me. "Wow," Artie says at last. "No wonder he's despondent. Poor bastard's still working the same shitty job he had when he was alive."

She's not stalled anymore, but moving hurriedly toward the room now, checking her watch.

They're not my sons anymore, but my documentarians. "A common mistake," the chaplain informs them when they all think I'm asleep, "is forgetting to ask for a physical reminder."

Robert and Artie stare.

"Of the loved one," she clarifies, gesturing my way.

I watch the boys through sparse eyelashes. Artie shakes his head. "Physical. Like what—a finger or toe?"

The chaplain ignores him, focusing on Robert. "A nice reminder might be a letter, drawing, or recorded voice message for the grandkids." She glances my way. "Or a thumbprint on some nice paper, if that's what she can handle."

Even a Jane Doe can manage that, with assistance.

A drawing. Again I recall the pretty crayon tree that my little Penelope made—and in she walks at last, her face set in sadness. No, no, don't be sad. My daughter has alternated between anger and melancholy for eleven days, since the doctors ended treatment and began palliative care: a decision that we all, unanimously, supported. I squint at the deep groove between her eyebrows. I smile for her.

She's not sad anymore, but suddenly fuming. "Where's Robby going?" she shouts, as her brother exits the room.

"Bathroom." Artie uses his thumbnail to pick his nose. Even while completing this disgusting and embarrassing gesture, she observes, he is smirking. "Have a good two-hour coffee break, Pen?" She can't look at him. She pushes a few flyaway hairs from her mother's clammy forehead, and her mother sighs deeply.

Her fingers coil in Mom's fragile hair as she recalls how, when her brother was ten and she twelve, she'd pinched his fingers in the hinge of a door. For a moment, before the grownups noticed what had happened, they'd stared at one another. Then he'd burst out laughing and she'd burst out crying. He infuriated her then; infuriates her now.

The machine flashes red. They exchange a glance. Robert is still gone. The alarm starts to sound and the nurses beat the doctors to the room (always there before the doctors, always there after the doctors). There is the iconic flat line, and their mother is gone too.

She's not a sister anymore, but a daughter. He's not a brother anymore, but a son. Buzz buzz buzz. Buzz. Buzz. Buzz. Hush. 4:17pm.

4:18. Penelope's eyes close. When she opens them again, she remembers the lollipop flowers: their scent, and the silk of their petals. Slowly, she removes her hand from her mother's hair—smoothing it as she does her own daughter's—and the anger drains, and a nurse guides her gently into a chair.

4:19.

4:20.

4:21.

4:22.

4:23. Robert returns. He rushes to the bed as Penelope and Artie step back and hospital staff take over. He gets in their way.

4:24.

4:25.

4:26—

The three comfort one another, simply by existing together, as close families do. Tidy sunlit room. Music and the littered sprawl of streets. Controversial clinics and parks. Rutabaga. Circo's Patisserie. Katy's Candy Store. Lovers and husbands, city and sky. Their mother is gone from her body, but still something remains—as buildings fall, and cities change, and nations shift their borders. As outside, the sun dims slightly on our world while another world churns beneath: steady, enormous, sensed but unseen.

OMGBRBLOLFDGB

OMG

Is what the driver's texting when, predictably, she rams her car straight into the Watsons' kitchen and our unit gets the call. "Been dispatched to the yellow house before," I tell Valerie. "It's close." By the time she stops nodding her head, I'm parking.

"Wow. It's really, really yellow."

I nod. "Last time, their scrawny little tree took the hit. City of Oakland put a guardrail up on that corner." I point through the windshield at three wide holes in the shoulder of the road. "Yanked it out last week for a safety upgrade." We lock eyes briefly, exiting the ambulance, but Val doesn't laugh so I don't either.

"Oh my god! Oh my god! Jesus!" a woman on the lawn is yelling.

"Is that the driver?" Val asks, and I say yeah, probably.

"Lordacardia," I add under my breath.

"What?"

"Her diagnosis. Tachylordyosis with the junctional Jesus."

"Got it." We stride across the grass.

Staring down at her intact body, the yelling woman pats herself all over as though she's lost her keys. A lot of them do this, if they're able. I'm fine, she reassures herself over and over as we approach: "I'm fine I'M FINE I'm fine." She pats her sides, her hips, her thighs, her ass. "Oh my god! Oh my god!

Jesus! I'm fine." This happens a lot too: it's like someone keeps hitting rewind on everything the patient says. I grin at Val.

"You appear to be fine," I agree, and the woman nods vigorously.

"I'm okay! I'm okay!"

"Not so much your car," I note, trying to snap her out of it.

It works. She goes mute and stares at her silver Toyota, which looks a little like a Coors can emptied and crushed by God. Then she stares at the gaping hole around it, in the Watsons' west-facing wall.

"Looks like nobody's home," Val says. It's just after 10 am: parents probably off at work in San Francisco, kids in school right down the block. "Everyone got lucky this time." "Not so much their house," the patient observes with a shaky smile at me. I lean forward to take a look through the hole, and Val escorts her slowly to the rig.

BRB

There's a lull after we've dropped the patient off, so we grab coffee. "I could fall asleep right here—take a little disco nap," I murmur in line at the café.

Val's face lights. "An EMS situation?"

I nod proudly. "That's right, young Padawan: earning money in our sleep." Val is drop dead gorgeous—long legs, plush lips, high tits. "What's this, your third day? Way to go with the lingo."

"I've got BOHICA down, too, for when we're slammed with calls. And 1 Dee 10: idiot." A few blond strands have escaped her ponytail. She brushes them up into her hat. "That one's kinda mean, though." She looks at me uncertainly.

Val's a good girl who moved out here from Idaho or someplace to save the city, so I'm holding back the nastier acronyms for later—AMMS, or acute Mexican mom syndrome, referring to hysterical screaming and easily adjustable to insult shriekers of any ethnicity; NFO, or normal for Oakland: a gunshot wound; APTFRAN, or apply pillow to face, repeat as necessary, indicating an annoying patient. I give her MAGGOT for now.

"M-A-G-G-O-T," she repeats diligently. "Medically able to go get other transportation." She squints as we approach the register, committing this new term to memory.

Once we've got our coffee, I hand mine over to Val. "Hang onto this. BRB. POC." I grin. "Pissing on the clock. And you should too, after me."

In the men's room I pull out the pewter flask my old partner gave me after our first bad call together: a high speed quad ejection that threw one patient at least a hundred feet. You'd think paramedics would avoid alcohol, as we see the damage it does firsthand—nope. Too much stress. And we get in drunken crashes, too, just like anyone. Kevin, who bought me the flask, is serving six in the Q now for gross vehicular manslaughter. When he gets out of San Quentin, he says, he's going to open a doughnut shop. I take a few nips.

It's not just us, either: I know more drug-addicted ER doctors and tequila-swilling nurses than I can count. Emergency medical workers need something to take the edge off—and I'm not talking about the suits in the adminiverse, here. I'm talking real medical workers, like the first on the scene when they lift the tractor-trailer off a patient and his organs slush back into his flat, tire-marked midsection. I'm talking the surgeon who reattaches a construction worker's toes, or the team that rolls up on a two-car MVA and fails to revive an infant in traumatic arrest.

Emerging from the men's room, I find Val chatting politely with some dick in a laptop bag. Whatever his job is—booking flights to London for his boss; making calls from this sunlit café—he probably thinks it's pretty important. He probably thinks the world will end if he doesn't meet a deadline. But soon Val won't give squares like him the time of day. Not even while she's just standing around, holding coffee.

Because while it's true that every job has its bullshit moments—like waiting with a corpse for hours on end until the cops get on the scene, or having to examine a patient who's clearly only suffering from incarceritis, the sudden onset of chest pains occurring upon arrest—being a paramedic is important. And like it or not, doing what we do reveals other jobs, and sometimes the people who hold them, to be unimportant. Trivial. Boring.

It was an argument I had over and over with my

fiancée. I didn't want to have dinner with her boring friends; didn't want to meet her boring boss. I wouldn't talk to her boring mother on the phone. So what? Did that make us incompatible? "It's like you can't be bothered to deal with anyone who isn't shot in the face," she'd say, "or laid out on the highway with a compound fracture."

"I deal with you," I'd say.

"I want more than to be dealt with. I want to be more important than fucking strangers. Than the assholes you work with, like Kevin."

"Really?" I'd say. "Kevin?"

She could be that way, my fiancée. Unnecessarily crappy. She knew what I meant; how I felt. How I'd take my own bullet to the face for her, or step onto the highway to shove her to safety. She knew I was better with actions with words—that, in my family, expressions of intimacy had consisted of Dad's drunken effusing and Mom's sad attempts to beat me black and blue while I pinned her struggling arms to her sides.

Even when she was leaving me, taking the engagement ring and two of my Earl Scruggs albums, I did whatever needed doing. I packed her pens and hair bushes, and a bunch of other little shit she'd forgotten. I labeled cardboard boxes. I loaded up a trailer and made two trips back and forth with her. And then I stood in the driveway, waving, while she pulled carefully onto the street for her final, solo trip.

When the trailer disappeared around the corner, I caught myself patting my body down as though I'd lost my keys. In my head I screeched "Oh my god! Oh my god! Jesus!"

Rejoining Val, I lift the coffees from her hands and give a curt smile. She excuses herself to the ladies' room, and for a moment Laptop and I face one another awkwardly as he rakes his eyes up and down my uniform, glaring like I'm a cock block. No, Laptop, it's not me. It's the job. This job will make a woman like Val look down on a man like you.

Unless she quits first. Because unlike my fiancée, whom I will soon remember to stop calling my fiancée, Val seems kind. Very kind, in fact, which worries me: you can't think of dying Santiago's mom as a loving mother—like any loving mother, like your own loving mother—when the kid's bleeding out on the sidewalk. You can't think of East Fourteenth's gun-toting teenagers as disenfranchised, beat down and shat on by the powers that be. And you can't think of an annoying patient as someone who's just very, very afraid. Then you'd start to feel afraid, too, and how the hell would you get through your shift? AMMS, I'll tell her when she's ready. NFO. APTFRAN.

I nod at Laptop, who nods back sulkily and heads toward an empty corner table. I watch him arrange his various cords and devices. You may eventually seal that big deal with the honchos in the Tokyo office, I'm thinking, but I'll resuscitate a toddler who's drowned in a creek.

LOLFDGB

By 6 pm, Val's relearned the lesson that our job is 5% blind panic, 5% bizarro world and 90% boredom. We've pushed an older gentleman's prolapsed anus back into place, argued with a fourteen-year-old about why Only Fools Skip School and hit another café for fresh coffee. But as we're settling down to drink, a real call comes in.

The wino's face is completely swollen with air that crackles under my fingertips when I palpate his cheek. I've seen this before—though generally after a forceful car accident, not a hobo street fight. Must've gotten hit hard in the chest a few times; maybe taken an unfortunate fall. *Sub Q air*, I scrawl: subcutaneous emphysema. I take his vitals, which are stable, and pass my notes over to Val.

Examining what I've written, she pulls me out of the rig with enormous eyes. "Stable? This guy is stable? Vital signs don't mean jack, do they?" she whispers.

"In his case, nope." I dart my eyes toward the homeless guy. "They can probably fix up his face, but this one's PCTTJ." Val flashes a quizzical look. "Patient care transferred to Jesus," I clarify, "also known as HBD." I pause for impact. "He be dead." She climbs back in the ambulance slowly and sits next to the patient. Her face looks strange, like she's forcibly keeping it together, so I decide to stick around for a minute.

"A few more questions," Val says. The guy nods and fidgets silently on the padded blue bench, staring everywhere but at her: into the front of the rig, up at the ceiling, down at the floor. He's only in his mid-fifties, and I can tell he's ashamed of being homeless; of having gotten in a fight with another homeless guy, and of taking up a pretty paramedic's time. And he should be. This one isn't dying from his injuries or the air that's blown his face up like a basketball, but from "a sip here, a sip there," as he admits grudgingly.

"You can't take a sip here or there," Val admonishes gently. Glancing over his pitted nose and yellow skin, she adds: "Not with cirrhosis of the liver." But alcoholics are fearless optimists. They believe, more than they ought to, in their bodies. He perks up as I linger between the open rear doors.

"You sound like Dr. Seuss," he says merrily; then, to me, "Doesn't she? 'You shall not sip it here or there! You shall not sip it anywhere!'" He laughs a wincing belly laugh. When I don't join in, he shrugs and goes back to watching the ceiling, oblivious to how rapidly he's approaching a state-run nursing home—then a lonelier, more final coffin. Val nods at me. Shutting the doors, I head up to the front of the vehicle.

In the emergency room the guy shakes our hands; thanks us for dropping him off, as though we're friends doing a favor. "No problem," I answer, heading for the exit. I've left my travel mug back in the Band-Aid box and want to enjoy it before it's completely cold.

"Good luck, Mr. Jenks." Valerie hustles to catch up with me.

Was that a formality, I'm wondering, or is she naïve enough to believe in luck for a goner like Jenks? The guy is CTD: circling the drain. But maybe her family back in Idaho only included the sort of functional alcoholics whose counterarguments don't involve uppercuts and jabs; who clean up once they find something to live for.

Reunited with our coffee, we smile. I clap her arm and let my hand linger as she stuffs more blond strands into her hat. If she's Goldilocks, I'll be Baby Bear's porridge. Not too hot. Not too cold. Juuust right, till she falls asleep in my bed. "You hanging in there? Eventful first week."

"Sure." She smiles lopsidedly; swipes at the hair that's already escaped across her forehead again. "This is exactly what I signed up for." I nod. "So what was up with his head?"

"The swelling?"

"Well, yeah." Her eyes go wide. "I mean I've heard of air leaking from the chest and getting trapped under the skin, but that was crazy. His head was a freaking asteroid. It made his face look tiny." She pauses, gaze drifting, and I prepare for her to wax poetic about alcoholism or homelessness or fistfights. Instead, she laughs. "*Oh ye of little face*! That's all I kept thinking, back there." She jerks a thumb toward the back of the rig. "It was so fucking hard not to crack up!"

I look closely at her then, turning in my seat to assess her as I did the yelling woman on the lawn; the old guy with the inside-out asshole; the teenager, high as a kite, with bruised forearms and the wino rising swollen from the sidewalk. She'll be okay, this one, I conclude. Maybe better than me. It's possible she will not require a pewter flask. "What?" she says, her eyes lit with a glittering amusement that changes her face entirely.

"Nothing." I look away.

The sun is leaving the sky now—just a tiny, vanishing hint of evening light CTD, circling the drain—and my fiancée appears to me as she does at this hour, eyes caught between anger and adoration, laying down her ultimatums. Me or Kevin. Me or the booze. Me or the job.

The sun was weak like this when she rolled down the driver's side window to hurl her parting comments. "Bye, Mike," she said coolly. "It's you or the booze now, you know, not me or the booze. You or the job. You or Kevin." Then she drove off and I stood there waving. Kevin? Really? Oh my god Jesus.

I return to the acronyms, shifting in my seat to feel the comforting discomfort of the flask jabbing my thigh. We drive aimlessly as I offer up APD, GDA and RT: acute Prozac deficiency, or depression; gonna die anyway, which is self-explanatory; room temperature, or already deceased. But the fun of the game is waning. Then the radio comes alive.

You or the booze. I steer through the streets, toward the highway and our new destination.

You or the job. Val stares blankly out the windshield.

You or Kevin. But I quiet my fiancée's ghost. LOLFDGB, I tell it silently, keeping my eyes on the road. Little old lady fall down go boom. OMG, I tell it. BRB.

MR. CHOMPERS

STELLA SAYS THE LIGHT in her bedroom is flickering; she wants me to stop folding the laundry and go up there with her. "No," I tell her. "You need to go upstairs yourself, and bring your pony back down. You dragged Mr. Chompers up there." I bend into the basket and excavate a shirt. It's her favorite: a pilly, green thing that transforms her into a frog. Ribbit, she shrieks, hopping, whenever I pull it over her misshapen face. Ribbit! Ribbit! I'm a frog. I fold the little shirt in half, and half again, while she lingers across the room. Outside, gray clouds glow as if backlit by a stronger sun than ours.

"Mama, I do not like that idea," she says. Her expression is divided between the urge to whine and the itch to run into my arms and demand that I change her into the frog shirt. I shoot her a look that means business.

"Stella, we've discussed this. If you'd like another Black Welsh for your stable, you need to be more responsible. You brought the pony upstairs. Why should I be the one to retrieve it?" Although Stella is only four, she's already reading chapter books. Black Pony Island is her favorite. She understands every word I've used.

"The light is flickering," she repeats. "It may explode"—pointing at the picture window behind me—"like a supernova." When I remain silent, she adds: "I will catch on fire."

"Is the light really flickering?" I transfer the frog shirt from my lap to the stack that I've started on the ottoman.

"Yes."

Like a frog's, Stella's ears and jaw are small; her eyes

large and round. She has no eyelashes, and due to a misaligned bite it's difficult for her to close her mouth. When we go out, people stare—the kids laughing or grimacing, the other mothers signaling Shhh and thanking whichever gods they thank for their own offspring's normalcy—but we go out regardless, every day, and I imagine that someday my daughter will set herself apart from her teenage friends by understanding why celebrities occasionally go insane, hiding in their houses to avoid the public eye.

"Right now? The light in your bedroom is flickering on and off, Stella?"

She tilts her head and places a finger on her afterthought of a chin, forgetting about the frog shirt as she decides whether to lie. The afternoon sky's blinding blankness presses up against the windowpane and I realize that our laundry can wait. Sometimes the sight of something desolate does that: reminds me to cherish my daughter's zeal. Our old couch sags as I stand (its firmness, like mine, long relinquished) and Stella's eyes light up. "Can we play now?" she asks as I take her tiny hand. We mount the stairs. I want to scoop her up and press her warmth into my breast, but instead I tell her that we won't be able to play until after I've fixed the bedroom light.

"And if it's not really broken," I say, "you'll have a time-out." Her face resumes the shape of indecision—then breaks into a grin. My daughter has calculated the time that it takes to fold a full basket of miniature shirts, pants, skirts, panties, tights, and socks and measured it against the ten minutes of silent time-out. If I had a husband, we'd exchange a look. She's too clever. We're in trouble.

At the top of the stairs, she pulls me toward her bedroom, where Mr. Chompers awaits. "Oh!" she'll say in a moment. "The light isn't on, because it's daytime. I think that the sky was flickering." I'll shake my head sternly; pretend disappointment, while brimming with the radiance of a sunlit cloud.

Last week, on the cheerful parking lot island outside a chain café, a little boy called my daughter a whore. We could've used the drive-through, but it was a sunny day, and there were giant green umbrellas over the outside tables, and Stella had wanted to sit. "Waterfalls," she'd sung out as we exited the café. Handing me her lemonade, she'd danced around a planter overflowing with blue lobelia.

The boy had stopped short, catching his mother's hand so that she paused, too, under the canvas awning. At first I'd thought he might dance with my daughter. But Stella is not the Cinderella for just any prince. I watched his eyes narrow as he took in her droopy features, her cleft lip— and I knew that he was about to scream something ugly. "Whore! You're a whore!" He glared at us. He was a very, very loud boy.

Afterward, Stella and I sat in hot metal chairs under a table with no umbrella. "It's like a heated car seat," she grinned, wiggling in her chair, "or a baked blueberry muffin." Then she made me tell her again what "whore" meant, and list some synonyms.

"Prostitute," I began. "Harlot, hooker, strumpet, tramp. Courtesan, hussy, painted woman, concubine."

Stella sipped her lemonade slowly. "A tramp is like a hobo, right? Do whores carry their things in a cloth bundle tied to a stick?"

"Sure, sometimes," I said, to say something. My head was still pulsing. With a mute and terrified glance, the mother had dragged her bellowing son immediately back to their car. Sometimes this happens: a little kid can't find the right insult when he wants to call Stella a monster and make her disappear.

My daughter's sneakered feet kicked at the leg of my toasty chair, tok tok tok tok tok. Her face was twisted in focused envisioning. "I don't have a good stick," she said. Then: "What colors are the painted women painted?"

People associate facial abnormality with mental deficiency—a deviance from the standard, the normal, the them. But Treacher Collins Syndrome, while characterized by deformity, doesn't signify cognitive delay. If I had a husband, I'd ask him whether he experiences the same mean pride that I do when Stella starts to speak. "My God!" strangers reply. "She knows the word 'despondent?'"

"Yes," I murmur humbly, giving her hand a little squeeze. And look at your kid. He just ate a fucking clod of dirt off the ground.

"Honey," I'd say to my hypothetical husband, "why isn't it enough for me that Stella's smart? Why do I need her to be smarter?"

"You're a mom," he might shrug, if he were a fabulous husband; or, if he were only average, "You're a competitive and slightly cruel person."

I don't have a husband, though, because Stella was conceived with a man I didn't know, back when I was proud of distinctly different things: fitting into teenagers' sizes at thirty; not being anchored by an ambitious career, a mortgage or a man; opening the driver's door to puke smoothly outside the car as I steered, at seventy miles an hour, around a curve by the Holland Tunnel. So perhaps my mean pride is an improvement.

Perhaps anything, in fact, is an improvement. While Stella sits perfectly still on the bed, condemned to boredom for an unbearable ten minutes, I recall more of the pointless, risky things that I did to distinguish myself from the standard, the usual; the them. First tat. Mescaline. Second tat. Reggie. Third tat: a cover-up for the first tat.

Now I earn the mortgage on our peeling yellow house by chatting up well-to-do parents in the upscale toy store that I manage. I still shop for clothing in the teenagers' section, but only because it saves money, which I'm setting aside for Stella's education. I'm free to live a mundane life now, because my daughter's birth separated me from them. "You have a mild form of TCS yourself, Raina" the first specialist told me. This was after he'd investigated my medical history and lab results, and I remember thinking that he pronounced my name weirdly, as though it were two separate words: Rain. Ah.

"What does that mean?" I asked, fingering my average-sized ears and proportional chin.

"Nothing much, in terms of your own life. You've done fine undiagnosed, and I suspect you'll continue to do fine." But then, as doctors will, Dr. Lloyd contradicted himself. "The one thing you may want to avoid—" and I grant him this much: he looked uncomfortable in that moment, waggling his fingers by his sides as though he'd just realized that what he was about to say would actually mean quite a bit, in terms of my own life "—is having any more children, or a grandbaby."

Then, unblinking, he watched my face become despondent. Morose. Glum. Melancholy. Woebegone, bitter, bereaved, cheerless, dejected, despairing, disconsolate, dismal, distressed, mournful, grieved, gloomy, doleful, downcast, forlorn, heartsick, languishing, low-spirited, sorrowful, lugubrious.

"Mama," Stella had said when we reviewed these synonyms, "why are there so many words for sad?"

We switched specialists last year, my daughter and I, but sometimes, ringing up a pregnant woman in the store, I remember Dr. Lloyd. I remember the guilty squirm of his blunt, liver-spotted hands as he explained that a grandchild would have only a fifty-percent chance at normalcy; that the severity of TCS unfolds exponentially, its symptoms worsening with every subsequent generation. "Rain. Ah." I whisper to myself, when I think of him administering his warning.

When the time-out is over, we have a little talk.

"Lying is bad," I tell Stella, who fidgets on her mahogany daybed. The sheets are cream; the blankets brown. If I had a husband, I'd high-five him for having avoided the pervasive Pink Fever.

"It affects American mothers at an alarming rate," he'd say, snuggling me, if he were fabulous. Then we'd start a running joke about how Stella's ecru-walled, adult bedroom was the real reason that her preschool teachers kept pulling us aside to tell us how she'd sung Nadir's aria from The Pearl Fishers to them, or how they'd overheard her explaining how a carburetor works to another child.

"She's an astounding girl," Miss Edna had gushed. "And you, a working single mom. What is it that you're doing with her at home?"

"Just the usual," I'd replied. Like any parent, whatever I do with my kid is the usual. I can't really envision any other way.

Now I run my fingers through Stella's moist curls. Always, on time-out, she sweats profusely, her impatience leaking through her glands. "Mama," she says slowly, when my smile signals her release, "isn't playing pretend like lying?"

"Yes," I say, "but without the intention to fool

anybody. That's the ethical difference." Stella understands what intention means—both linguistically and experientially. She may be the strongest-willed person I know.

"Because everyone knows playing is fake?"

"Because everyone knows playing is fake."

She looks at me, considering. Spittle escapes from her little froggy mouth, and I wipe it away with a finger. "You like me," she concludes, "but you don't like to stop folding laundry." The gleam through the window is dimming now. Soon, we'll have to drag Mr. Chompers back downstairs so that Stella can eat her dinner.

"I do like to stop folding laundry," I correct her. "Stelly, there is nothing I would rather do than play with you and Mr. Chompers. I like that his stable overlooks the Dead Sea. I like the fact that his best friend is a bear who makes pancakes. But the laundry still needs to get folded."

As she chews this over, I devise an equation for beauty. I don't mean this in the Pythagorean sense, or any aesthetic sense at all, but rather in a scientific one, like the equation for cellular respiration or the equation for photosynthesis: an equation that explains a reaction. When I look at Stella, my ribs expand and the color of the world brightens. When strangers look at her, their throats close. So how long, then, would it take the average stranger to experience Stella as a person, and then an intellect, and then a beauty? Length of time equals degree of normalcy divided by breadth of mind. Eight days of sustained engagement on average, I calculate, or a month of infrequent exposure.

Stella is laughing wildly. She's bucked herself right off of Mr. Chompers, and lies twisted on the slate gray carpet. "What happened?" I shout, in mock alarm.

"He saw a Pegasus soaring fast fast fast in the sky, and he tried to fly too." She flaps her arms, herky-jerky.

"And?"

"Mama." She swats at my question and rolls her lashless eyes. "Mr. Chompers doesn't have wings." I nod slowly at the veracity of this statement, conceding to Stella's logic, as she gathers invisible flowers in an imaginary basket. She sorts through them; presents one to me. "Feed this to Mr. Chompers," she says. "It's safe, with no hallucinogenic poison." She's been reading the botany book again. The window is darkening quickly now, emanating a creeping chill. I find myself staring at her unusual contours: the nose that Dr. Lloyd had suggested reconstructing in sixteen years; the jaw he'd advised us to alter in five.

Stella notices my somber inspection and puts both hands flat on her cheeks. We regard one another quietly in the tasteful, muted bedroom whose reflection powers up in the windowpane as the sunlight powers down. Finally she lets her hands drop, retrieves the chimerical flower from my open palm, and feeds it to Mr. Chompers. I regain myself and scratch at his polyester chin, which she tells me he likes quite a bit. Smiling at my attentiveness to her pet, she says: "Sometimes fake is better than real. I mean, way lots of better. Lots." She nods the pony's head up and down, up and down in agreement.

Ugly [uhg-lee], adjective: unpleasant to look at; offensive to the sense of beauty.

If I had a husband, he wouldn't necessarily be handsome. I had my share of pretty men, back in the day. But he would be beautiful—meaning, when my mother reminded me that I ought to learn to cook, he'd put his hand on her shoulder and say: "Mrs. Owens, all that I want her to make for me is perfectly square ice cubes. I love to cook. The kitchen is my domain." And when the neighbors looked askance at our weedy front yard, he'd paint us a sign reading "530 Martin Luther King Boulevard: Where Plants Go to Die," and hammer it into the ground.

You see, when Stella came along I had to retool my mental lexicon. Husband means something different now. Parent, too, and child. And appropriate and intelligent and right. And of course, normal has completely changed – and beauty, I'm still figuring out. But I can tell you exactly what ugly means. Ugly is crystal clear now.

Ugly [uhg-lee], adjective: threatening trouble or danger. Morally revolting. Mean. Well, she's out, I think to myself when the monitor goes silent. Someday I'll throw the thing away, but not yet.

"What's that?" Stella asked me once, pointing at the

little square of plastic.

"It's a baby monitor."

"Do you use it to monitor babies?"

"That's a sensible conclusion," I answered, "but no. I use it to eavesdrop on you when you're sleeping."

"I see," she said rather severely, and then: "I should probably get one too, to eavesdrop on you. But I want the kind that's a lizard."

The monitor alerts me to Stella's every move. One rustle of the blanket, and it speaks hoarsely in my ear. Half of a nocturnal utterance, Ma, and its little red signal flashes in the dark. Someday I'll trust Stella to breathe easily through the night—but not quite yet. Soon, I tell myself, I'll forget about Dr. Lloyd. Soon I'll think only of Dr. Varner, who pronounces my name correctly and understands how deeply his prophecies affect patients, in terms of their own lives.

Dr. Lloyd told me that, whereas Stella's ears are very small, my grandchild's would likely be absent. Dr. Varner tells me that my daughter has excellent hearing. Dr. Lloyd told me that I should forget the college fund and save my money to "restore Stella's face to a more typical structure." Dr. Varner tells me that her eyesight is enviable. Dr. Lloyd told me that two primary concerns in individuals with TCS are the ability to breathe and to eat. Dr. Varner urges me to throw the monitor away: Stella's breathing is completely normal. And yes, I used to rail against normalcy, but understand this: in a medical specialist's office, there is nothing better to hear than "normal," especially when it's followed by "life expectancy."

If I had a husband, he would've tossed the monitor out by now—or donated it to a family in need, if he were fabulous. At any rate, he'd be helping me shake the anxious feeling with which I listen during her afternoon naps, and through the long dark nights. But I don't have a husband, so the monitor and I keep tabs. For now, we're the perfect couple: its scratchy voice calms me, and we light up together when she speaks in her sleep.

Mr. Chompers clamped in my armpit, I fill a glass of water in the kitchen sink. I pad into the living room and ease onto our deflated couch. Then, in a spurt of faith, I turn the monitor facedown on the coffee table, hiding its little red light: A start, I think, satisfied.

A sly breeze sneaks in through the walls somehow, and I drop the pony to the floor. It slumps against my leg as I resume my folding. Overall, it's in pretty bad shape: it reeks of sour spit, having served for several years as Stella's naptime pillow, and its black coat is ragged where I trimmed it after a glue incident. I should sew up its leg, I remind myself, eyeing the spot where its rear haunch is ripped, white filling bulging from the wound. Then I admonish myself for thinking of Mr. Chompers as an it.

He came to us as an adoptee, my daughter's steadfast Black Welsh—brought home from the toy store when he failed to sell. Somehow, I'd known she would love him. But why? I fold one last sock into its mate and toss the pair onto the ottoman. It rolls across and lands on the rug, but I don't chase it. I squint my eyes and stare at Stella's trusty steed, trying to run my new equation on him. How long will it take me to see Mr. Chompers as beautiful? Four minutes? Maybe five?

A quarter-hour passes as Mr. Chompers rests, sullenly, under my scrutiny. Eventually I become sullen too. I shift on my drooping perch. And just when I decide that the equation must be faulty, that I will never fully understand beauty—adorableness, charm, allure, bloom, attraction, glamour, grace, pulchritude—and that its formulae cannot be applied to a stuffed animal, the pony winks his glass eye coyly.

Startled, I rise, knocking a small stack of Stella's superhero panties to the floor. Mr. Chompers snorts in glee; a sound both noble and playful. He's a charmer, I see now. A gentlemanly pony. I approach him and lay a timid hand on his back. When he nuzzles my shoulder, I scritch at his chin. This is it, I'm thinking as he whinnies. I've gone insane.

If I had a husband, he'd step around the ottoman and hug me tightly; ask whether I might've ingested one of Stella's invisible, hallucinogenic flowers. Or, if he were fabulous, he'd simply join us—Mr. Chompers and me—in watching the walls of our modest home dissolve. I walk up the stairs to Stella, who sleeps curled in her bed, and I think: there are an infinite number of solutions to the equation.

"Are blue whales morose?" my daughter asks in her sleep, opening one eye just a little bit. Then, swatting her own silly pun away: "Nooooo."

Together, the pony and I watch. Stella giggles, and

her beauty blossoms exponentially, like microorganisms in a culture; like our human population; like ions in an electrical field. And we are in that electrical field now, the pony and Stella and I—the house dissolved into a field of pretend wildflowers, where a friendly bear flips pancakes and nothing stands still. Far above, golden clouds crash together like cymbals around the sun. Red petals roll in a vivid Mediterranean wave, and I nod slowly to Mr. Chompers.

"Just look. Look at her," I say.

ACKNOWLEDGEMENTS

"She Must Remember," a top-ten finalist in the Zoetrope: All-Story short story contest, first appeared in *The New Guard* (2011); "Zero Pressure," named a Notable Story by the story South Million Writers Award, first appeared in *Carve Magazine* (Summer 2009); "Flyaways" first appeared in *Glimmer Train* (issue 96); "Mr. Chompers" was first published in *ZYZZYVA* (issue 101).

SOMA MEI SHENG FRAZIER is an East Coast native living in the San Francisco Bay Area. This is Soma's second chapbook of stories. Her debut fiction collection, *Collateral Damage: A Triptych*, earned praise from Nikki Giovanni, Daniel Handler (a.k.a. Lemony Snicket), Antonya Nelson, Sarah Shun-lien Bynum, Molly Giles, and others—and won the RopeWalk Press Editor's Fiction Chapbook Prize. You can find her work online in publications, including *Eclectica Magazine*, *Carve Magazine*, *Eleven Eleven*, Kore Press, and *Glimmer Train* (bulletin 72, also featuring Anthony Doerr and Kate Gale). New work is forthcoming in *Glimmer Train* and *ZYZZYVA*.